THE INVISIBLE HARRY

Marthe Jocelyn

•

The Invisible Harry

illustrated by **Abby Carter**

DUTTON CHILDREN'S BOOKS • New York

Library of Congress Cataloging-in-Publication Data

Jocelyn, Marthe.
The invisible Harry/by Marthe Jocelyn; illustrated by Abby Carter.
p. cm.
Summary: Despite her mother's edict against pets in the apartment,
eleven-year-old Billie is unable to resist a homeless puppy and enlists the
help of her scientific friend Jody in making the little dog invisible.
ISBN 0-525-46078-0 (hc)
[1. Dogs—Fiction. 2. Science—Experiments—Fiction. 3. Schools—Fiction.
4. New York (N.Y.)—Fiction. 5. Humorous stories.]
I. Carter, Abby, ill. II. Title.
PZ7.J579Ir 1998 [Fic]—dc21 98-33507 CIP AC

Published in the United States 1998 by Dutton Children's Books,
a division of Penguin Putnam Books for Young Readers
345 Hudson Street, New York, New York 10014
http://www.penguinputnam.com/yreaders/index.htm
Printed in U.S.A.
First Edition
1 3 5 7 9 10 8 6 4 2

For Tom

M. J.

For Carter and Samantha,
and our dog, Willie

A. C.

CONTENTS

THE INVISIBLE HARRY

1 • *The Offer*

*T*he phone rang. I was at the kitchen table, eating peanut butter on a rice cake really slowly, so that it would be time for supper before I'd even started my homework. My mother's hands were wet, rinsing the broccoli, so I answered the phone.

"Hello?"

"Hi, it's me. Did you do the homework yet?"

"Who's on the phone, honey?" asked my mother.

I turned my back. Who appointed *her* the phone monitor?

"Hi, Hubert," I said to my best friend. "Uh, no. I haven't started yet. Why?"

"You know the history assignment? The coat of arms? The one we have to create for our own family?"

"Yeah?"

"The word is 'yes,' " said my mother.

"Do you think this is good?" asked Hubert. "I'm going to use a Chinese dragon, you know, for my heritage. And a ship, because that's how we got here. And I need something else, to symbolize me. What do you think?"

"You should use a package of Banana Bubbalot Gum," I said.

"Billie, that's perfect! You're so smart sometimes! What are you going to do?"

"Probably a cracked heart, for my heritage, for my broken home." I noticed my mother had no comment on that statement. "And, I don't know what other stuff yet."

"How about a book?"

"A book isn't exactly thrilling," I said.

"Isn't it about time to start doing your homework instead of just talking about it?" asked my mother.

"I have to go, Hubert," I said. "See you tomorrow."

I hung up. The rice cake was gone. I opened my binder. I rearranged the pencils in their pencil loops. The phone rang.

Lucky for me, my mother's hands were wet again, rinsing the basmati rice.

"Hello?"

"Hi, is this Billie?"

"Uh-huh."

"Hi! It's Jody! I haven't talked to you for so long! How was your summer? Do you even remember me?"

"Sure." How could I forget?

"Who's on the phone, honey?"

I turned my back and hunched over.

"Oh, my God, I had to go away on a nightmare vacation with my parents to the shopping capitals of Europe. The only good part was going to the Museum of Science and Industry, in Paris. Um, anyway, do you remember my dog, Pepper?"

"Of course."

"Well, Pepper had an adventure out in the world. She ran away one night, and I was going completely crazy walking around the streets calling and calling her name. I even phoned the police to see if anyone had reported a dead dog, but it turns out that she was just off having a good time, and about a month ago, she had puppies!"

"Puppies!"

My mother glanced up. "In your dreams . . ." she murmured.

I dropped my voice to a whisper. "How many?"

"Three of the cutest little furballs you ever saw. My mother is having a nervous breakdown. Of course she never bothered to realize that Pepper was a girl, and suddenly her closet turns into a birthing room. She opened the door one morning and there was Pepper, curled up on Mom's tangerine cashmere sweater, licking her pups."

Listening to Jody is like hearing someone talk in Fast Forward. She uses up words at twice the pace of anyone else.

"Anyway," she kept on going, "my cousin Amy is hopefully taking one of them, if her brother's not allergic, and there's a kid at school who might . . . but I was wondering if you might want the other one?"

"Oh, yes, totally!" My brain was letting off sparks, I was trying to think so fast. "I'm going to call you back, okay? I just have to work things out."

"Is that code for begging your mother?"

"Uh-huh." I dropped my voice to the slightest whisper. "But save one for me, okay? I'll call you in a couple of days." I hung up quickly. I flung open my books in a fever of industry.

I've been dying to have a pet for about five years. My sister, Jane, doesn't count, even though she spends a portion of every day down on her knees, panting or whinnying.

A dog would be best, but a cat would be okay. I'm not going to be ridiculous and ask for a horse or a monkey.

Apparently someone gave me a goldfish the summer Jane was born, and I forgot to feed it and it turned belly-up; my mother has told me

ever since that I am not old enough to be responsible for another living creature. Plus I
guess she doesn't want me to be.

The last time I tried the pet subject with my
mother, I didn't get very far.

"Well," she said, "I suppose we could get a
toad. It would be useful for eating the cockroaches."

"Mom, we don't have cockroaches. I've seen
one about twice in my life."

"Well, then, it wouldn't be fair to the toad,
would it? The poor toad would starve to death
here. Sorry, no toads."

"Mom! I don't want a toad! I want a dog!"

"I'll be happy to get a dog, as soon as we
move to a farm."

And guess what? We don't have any plans to
move to a farm.

But now Jody was offering me a puppy!
Free, and no doubt really cute. Pepper is white,
sort of a terrier, with brown freckles all over her
nose.

"Who had puppies?" asked my mother.

"Oh, uh . . ." I couldn't even lie and say

"some kid from school," because my mother is the librarian at our school, and she knows every kid and every parent and probably every dog who goes there.

"Uh, a friend of Hubert's family," I said.

"Nothing better than a new puppy for messing up your life," said my mother, looking me straight in the eye. "I'm so glad we don't have to deal with that."

2 • *Duping Dad*

My dad lives in an apartment way uptown, over near the Hudson River. He moved there four years ago when my parents decided that "till death do us part" was too long to wait. They parted so they wouldn't have to yell at each other anymore. And now my mother can barely trust him to have us for a weekend. She thinks we'll have too much fun and want to live with him all the time.

Dad's apartment is very small, but the building is fancy, compared to our loft downtown. To begin with, there's a doorman who wears a navy blue uniform with gold epaulets and brass buttons. He looks almost royal, and his name is Octavio, which sounds more like an Italian duke than a doorman.

Octavio always pretends to be surprised when we visit, like he hasn't seen us in two years instead of two weeks, and we've grown so much that we're ready for college or something.

But he's funny, and he twirls his mustache at Jane and carries our bags all the way into the elevator as if we need help. Then he tells our father how lovely we are, and my dad tries to get us upstairs before Octavio pulls out the photographs of his two round sons. He thinks we're going to marry them someday.

The elevator is lined with gleaming wood and has stars painted on the ceiling, as if the passengers are on a voyage to outer space. My dad lives on the eleventh floor.

He has a living room, a kitchen, a bathroom, a bedroom, and a balcony about the size of a bathtub. The sofa in the living room folds out into a bed, and that's where Jane and I have to sleep when we stay with him every other weekend.

This time, Dad was getting an extra night because my mom was going to the American Librarians' Conference. He would have to take us to school on Monday, all the way from uptown, and stay at our loft on Monday night.

I hate sharing a bed with Jane. She is a wiggler and a blanket hog. She claims that I talk in my sleep. But neither of us wants to sleep on the floor, which is what my father always suggests when we complain.

Dad hit the button on the answering machine almost as soon as we walked in the door, just like he always does. Instead of a beep, his machine has a little whistle, like a baby's toy.

Click. Whirr. Whistle.

"Hello, Alex." It was my mother's voice. "I guess you're still out for supper. I just wanted to say good night to the girls."

"Mommy!" squealed Jane. "I want to talk to Mommy!"

"I'm going to a movie with Susan so I won't be here later," her voice continued.

"Oh, no!" Jane threw herself on the couch in a sulk.

"I'll talk to them in the morning before I leave for the conference. I'll be back around noon on Tuesday. Please remind them to brush their teeth at least once while they're with you."

My dad rolled his eyes.

"Good night, Jane, honey, be a good girl."

"Okay, Mommy." Jane decided to be brave.

"Good night, Billie."

Click. Whirr. Whistle. New message.

"Er, yes, Alex, this is Phil here."

"Uh-oh," my dad said.

". . . Look, the graphic you did yesterday looks terrific, really terrific . . ."

"*But,*" said my dad.

"But," said Phil's voice, "believe it or not, the client has changed the name of the product, as of last night, and wants the whole job ready with the new name in time for the presentation on Monday morning. I know this is inconvenient, but I'm going to have to ask you to come in tonight and do it. Sorry and thanks. See you Monday, pal."

Click. Whirr. Whistle.

"Pal?" My dad was shouting at the answering machine.

"Pal?" He stuck out his tongue at the blinking light. "My kids are here for the weekend, pal, and we rented *E.T.*, and we were going to eat junk food and not brush our teeth, and now I have to go into the office and work, just because some dumb guy changed the name of his product?"

"Oh, Daddy," cried Jane, "it's not fair! Do you have to?"

He slumped onto the sofa and sighed in a gust. "Yes, sweetie, I have to. That man, Phil, is the boss at my job. I have to do everything he says until it's my turn to be boss."

He moaned as he stood up. "I guess I'd better call Mrs. Ewing in 8B, to see if she can come up and sit with you."

"Dad! She's about ninety years old!"

"And she's smelly," added Jane, "like moss."

"Well, how about Octavio? He'd probably be thrilled to let you watch TV in his office."

I was about to put in a plea for being old enough to look after Jane myself, when a brilliant plan wafted into my head like a breeze from an open window.

"You know, Dad, there's this new girl we've been wanting to try out as a baby-sitter, only Mom never goes anywhere. And she actually lives uptown. And she's really smart and scientific. Her name is Jody, and she's fifteen or sixteen. Definitely old and responsible."

Dad jumped on the idea.

"Well, do we know her phone number?"

"In my backpack."

As I went to find it, I was thinking how my mother would have asked forty questions, like, How exactly do we know this person? and, How long have we known her? and, What is her last name? and, What do her parents do? and, Does she smoke cigarettes?

But when my father sees the quick solution

to a problem, he doesn't bother with possibly disturbing details.

Of course, even my mother would probably not think to ask, Does this girl have any unusual hobbies? Can she make things disappear?

3 • *Puppy Love*

While we were waiting for Jody to get there, I started to worry about what she might be wearing. I'd only actually seen her once, and her clothes would have to be described as Beyond Weird.

I could have hugged her when she came in. She had on jeans and a sweatshirt, and her braces glinted like jewels in her mouth. She looked like a regular person. She was carrying a big canvas bag that she slipped off her shoulder and swung to the rug behind the couch.

"I brought my homework, Mr. Stoner. I hope that's all right with you. I thought that after

Jane and Billie go to bed I could work a little on my essay."

"Oh, certainly, Jody. That's fine. I'm hoping I won't be gone past ten or ten-thirty, but you just never know in these situations."

Jody put on a look as if these situations came along all the time and she was well-equipped to handle them.

"Don't worry about a thing, Mr. Stoner. Is there anything you want to tell me about bed-time or anything?"

She followed him into the hall where he was putting on his jacket. I could hear him mumbling instructions, making them up on the spot. He's not too good at enforcing rules. He thinks we'll forgive him for not living with us if we stay up late and eat a thousand sour cream and onion potato chips when we sleep over at his place.

"Billie!" Jane whispered urgently.

"What?"

"There's something alive in here!" She was kneeling beside Jody's bag, fumbling for the zipper. Sure enough, the bag shifted.

"Jane! Wait! It's not ours. Wait till Dad leaves!" I had a delicious suspicion. "Jane! Don't touch it!"

The bag was definitely moving.

I dragged Jane into the hallway before she could say another word.

"Good-bye, Dad! Don't work too hard!"

He smiled and apologized again and ruffled our hair and said thanks to Jody and finally shut the door.

Jody put her finger to her lips and whispered, "Two-minute rule . . . Don't say anything for at least two minutes, in case he has to come back."

We stood huddled by the door, waiting to hear the *ting* of the elevator. Jane held her breath. Even Jody was quiet, and that's really a feat.

"Okay, come on!" Jody turned back into the living room, and Jane dashed ahead, straight to the breathing shoulder bag. She unzipped the zipper, and we both squealed at once.

The puppy poked his nose out, sniffing. I felt dizzy, he was so beautiful. He was clearly de-lighted to be free. He tried to get his paws up, but the bag kept collapsing on him and he couldn't get out. He was only about as big as one of my father's shoes. His fur was the color of French vanilla ice cream, freckled and speckled with chocolate spots. He had sticky-uppy ears with silky tips, and big brown eyes.

"Ooooh, he's so cute!" Jane tried to grab him, so I stepped in front of her.

"Hey!" she cried, but I stood my ground.

"Cool it, guys," said Jody, sounding like a grown-up. "You'll scare him."

"Sorry, Jane," I muttered. My cheeks were burning. "You can hold him first. But sit down, and be careful!"

Jane obediently sat and crossed her legs. Jody picked up the puppy and put him into Jane's lap. He immediately started to chew her shirt.

"Hey!" scolded Jody. "No nipping!" She held his mouth closed for a moment. "He's just a baby," she explained to us. "He's teething and wants to gnaw on everything."

"What's his name?" whispered Jane, stroking his back with fingers like feathers.

"He doesn't have a name yet," said Jody.

"I've been calling him Boy, because he was the only boy in the litter."

His tail was wagging back and forth, and he kept sniffing us with curious sniffs.

"Maybe we can help think of a name," said Jane. I never saw her be so gentle as when she patted him.

I put my nose right up to his, just touching at the tips.

"Woof," I whispered. Pant, pant, he whispered back.

He licked me with a big, slobbery kiss across my nostrils.

And then a loud click announced a key in the front door. Jane clutched the puppy as her eyes went wide.

4 • The Idea

Hide him!" whispered Jody.

The blanket Dad had left for our bed was on the couch. I flung it across the puppy in Jane's

lap and pulled her down into a reclining hug.

"Hey, Dad!" I said, meeting his eyes. My smile was supposed to hide the fact that I felt like throwing up.

"We're playing hospital. Jane is a baby, abandoned by a downtrodden victim of society."

"Uh-huh," said Dad, hardly glancing at us. "I forgot the keys to the office." He scooped them up from the table and slid them into his pocket.

The puppy's nose started to explore, making the blanket shake.

Then, "Ow! Ow! Owwww!" Jane cried out. "He bit me!"

She clutched at her stomach, bunching the blanket and snorting.

"Are you okay, sweetie?" Dad asked.

"She's a really good actor," Jody piped up. "She's just getting into her character."

"I'll see you in the morning, then, girls. Have fun!"

"Bye, Daddy!"

He was gone again. Jane tore off the blanket and lifted the puppy up to look him in the face.

"Bad doggy!" she said. "It's your turn, Billie.

I'm mad at him." I moved my knees closer to her for the transfer.

He was so warm and little, I could feel his heart beating through his chest. My own heart turned over with a bump. His paws were big and goofy, like he was wearing those joke animal slippers that double your foot size. His fur was like a baby's hair or dandelion floss.

"Jane," said Jody, "why don't you get him a drink of water after his ordeal?"

"What should I put it in?" asked Jane, hopping to her feet in a flash.

"Use one of the cereal bowls," I suggested. "You know, with the blue stripe."

She scurried away to the kitchen.

"So," said Jody, as if she'd been waiting for us to be alone. "Did you ask your mother? Can you keep him?"

"She doesn't want a pet," I said, feeling forlorn as my fingers rested on the puppy's silky head. "She just doesn't. It's as simple as that."

"That stinks," said Jody. "But it's typical of a parent. To say no without even trying. They always accuse us of not trying, like with

Gorgonzola cheese or something disgusting, but really they're the ones with rigid rules. You're only asking to love an animal. My mother is just the same way. She lets Pepper live with us because my dad was the one who got her, but the puppies? Forget it. I'm just going to have to make them disappear somewhere. . . ."

"Disappear? You mean really disappear?"

"Well, actually, I meant 'go away,' you know, to a shelter or a pet shop, but now that you mention it . . ." Her eyes got bright, and she grinned a big, shiny grin.

"How much do you think your mother would mind having a pet she couldn't see?"

5 • *Harry Houdini*

Jane came inching back into the room, trying to keep the bowl level.

"Is the puppy hungry, Jody?" she asked eagerly. "Can we feed him? What does he like to eat?"

"I brought him some of his PuppySnack, Jane, if you want to give him a treat." Jody pulled a foil package out of her shoulder bag and gave it to Jane.

"Just one or two, though. We don't want him to get sick."

"I'm hungry, too," said Jane as she watched the puppy chomp on his cookie.

I went to Dad's kitchen and found the potato chips and some cheddar cheese and green grapes. We had a picnic on the floor while the puppy tried to climb our knees.

Jody told us about her project for the science fair.

"After countless experiments with layers of reflective substances, I developed a formula for solar popcorn. It really works, too, except that it takes about two hours of serious sunshine to get a bowl of popcorn, and most people don't think about snacking that far in advance. But it works, so I'll probably win."

I crumbled cheese in my fingers and let the puppy lick it off.

I told Jody about the medieval pageant we

were preparing for at school. We'd been making the costumes for weeks in art, painting tabards on brown paper and forming shields out of papier-mâché and hooking together soda pop caps for chain mail.

"It sounds mighty," said Jody. "We never have fun at our school. 'It's too distracting from the serious matter of education.'" She was imitating someone I was glad not to know.

"Oh, my God, it's late, Jane. What if your dad comes home and you're not even in your pajamas? It's after nine-thirty! You have to go to bed!"

Jane immediately performed her finest imitation of a sick cat, but Jody insisted that the puppy was tired and had to go to sleep right away. She took him into the bathroom and closed the door.

I lay down next to Jane on the sofa bed and snuggled her the way my mother does if she can't get to sleep. This means that she tucked her freezing cold feet between my legs and used my arm for an extra pillow. I sang "Hush, Little Baby" until she told me to shut up because my breath was tickling her ear. When she finally fell asleep, I had to take my arm out from under her head in the most careful maneuver possible.

Jody was sitting on the floor of the bathroom, reading one of my dad's *Fine Home Building* magazines. I don't know when he thinks he's going to build a fine home, but he has enough issues to wallpaper the bathroom.

The puppy was asleep on the mat, curled up like a dog on a greeting card.

"Well?" asked Jody. "Are you ready? Should we do it? I have the powder in my bag. You know it works."

That's for sure. I am an expert in that department. The way I met Jody was because I found her makeup bag in Central Park. Before I found her to give it back, I tried the powder in the compact, and, believe it or not, I disappeared. I'm not kidding, I swear. I totally vanished. It was one of Jody's secret formulas. She is a science genius.

And being invisible was amazing. For one thing, I went outside in New York City by myself! The hard part was not being able to tell anyone, except Hubert. And I sort of missed my mother after a while.

But that wouldn't bother a dog. . . .

"Ummm," I said, "I'm thinking. . . ."

It was just too easy. My mother wouldn't have to know for a while. By then, I could prove that I'm ready to have a pet. I could keep it in my room and take it for walks. I could even take it to school. I could buy food with my allowance. And I would have this sweet, fuzzy dog baby for my very own.

"Okay," I said. "Go for it!"

"Hurrah!" whooped Jody. "I love a brave move." She dove into her bag and pulled out her makeup case.

"Ooooh!" I cried in recognition.

Jody smiled at me. "Feeling nostalgic?" she asked.

"Wait a minute!" I had thought of something. "What about, you know, what about, um . . . poop? Is the poop invisible? And how am I going to know when he wants to go?"

"He's almost totally trained," Jody assured me. "He'll mostly only do it outside, on the curb. And I remember with Pepper, when I was testing the stuff on her, the poop stays invisible until it, uh, cools off. About two minutes. Then you can see it, and you just use newspaper or a bag, like with a regular dog. I'll give you the rest of the PuppySnack, so you're set."

I rubbed my nose between his ears and gave the little speckled nose a good-bye kiss. Then, I sat back on my heels, giving Jody room to work. She was swift and efficient. Using toilet paper as a tool, she daubed powder across the puppy's head, around his fluffy neck, and then down his body and tail.

Within seconds, he went all shimmery, just the way it had been with me. It was like I was wearing my mom's reading glasses. And a minute later, he was gone, and we were looking at Dad's royal blue bathroom carpet where my new pet used to be.

"Hey," said Jody as she put away her equipment, "you never picked a name."

I reached out to make sure he was still there. When my fingers found him, I stroked his invisible back.

"I think I'll call him Harry," I whispered, feeling a bit awed by the magic. "After the greatest disappearing magician of all time, Harry Houdini. His name is Harry."

"That's good," said Jody. "Harry."

We decided to get into ready-position in case Dad came home. Harry woke up when I moved him to the sofa bed, and he began to whimper. While I put on my pajamas, he kept on whining and crying.

"Why are you so sad, little guy?" I patted his furriness, telling him that everything would be okay.

"Maybe he misses his mother," suggested Jody.

"What should we do?"

"In the books they say to put him in a cozy place and put a clock next to him. The ticking is supposed to sound like a dog mother's heartbeat."

I glanced around the apartment.

"The only clock my father has is the digital clock radio next to his bed."

Jody laughed. "Somehow I don't think that Z-100 will perform the same service."

"I know!" I said. I lay down on the sofa bed with my back to Jane, and Harry snuggled on my chest, under the blanket. He stopped crying almost at once. He felt like a hot water bottle and a teddy bear in one. I was in heaven.

Jody sat on the floor with a biography of Marie Curie across her knees. I guess I dozed off. I vaguely remember Jody saying good-bye. I remember Dad telling her she was a real find and that we'd call her again soon.

And I remember thinking that Harry's snuffles were the sweetest sound I'd ever heard.

6 • The Brunch Test

Hi! My name is Patrick, and I'm your waiter this morning! Eggs Florentine is the brunch special today, along with freshly baked pumpkin muffins. Can I get you some coffee to start, sir?"

My dad ordered cappuccino, and I got orange juice. Jane had to get water because she hates those little pip things in fresh-squeezed juice, which is the only kind you can get at the places Dad takes us. Then I thought about Harry in the backpack at my feet, and I ordered an extra water.

Of course, getting Harry into the backpack had been a bit of a challenge.

In my first conscious minute, I felt him lick my face and knead my chest with his paws and flap his tail back and forth across my arm like a flyswatter. This is a lot of activity to wake up to. Especially to pretend that all this motion was coming from me.

Jane was rubbing her eyes and watching me with curiosity. It would be a disaster for Jane to know about Harry.

I put a pillow over her face and used the three seconds before she pulled it off, screaming, to leap from the bed with Harry in my arms and head for the bathroom, dragging my backpack full of clothes with my foot.

While I was getting dressed, I could hear Harry's panting, as regular as a raspy clock. I fed him most of the PuppySnack. And just while I was wondering if I could teach Harry to pee in the toilet, I stepped in a puddle and realized he had taken care of the problem for this morning. "*Almost* totally trained," I heard Jody's voice in my head. "*Mostly* only outside." It took half a roll of toilet paper (and six flushes) to dry the floor.

Harry was very involved in the cleanup. He kept bumping into me and getting caught between my feet. Soggy bits of toilet paper, stuck to Harry's paws, seemed to be dancing by themselves on the tiles.

Then suddenly, he made a weird little growl in his throat, and I smelled something I hope never to be quite so close to again.

"Harry!" I moaned. But I couldn't move because I didn't know where he'd made the drop. I sat as still as the toilet until I could see a faint pile of poop appearing under the sink—thankfully nowhere near the rug.

"Billie!" wailed Jane. "It's my turn."

"One second!"

I took another roll of paper from the cupboard and scooped the mound into the toilet. One final flush, and one long spray of Natural Citrus Atomizer to clear the air.

"That was completely disgusting, Harry," I scolded in a whisper.

He whimpered.

I cleaned off his paws and picked him up. "But I still love you." I rolled my cheek against his dear invisible ears and then shoveled him into my pack, despite the feet going every which way. I left the top zipper open in case he wanted to poke his face out. It seemed like he was little enough to fit with room to spare.

I could have eaten breakfast four times by the time the drinks came. I don't know why we can't just have cereal at Dad's house, but this brunch thing is his idea of living it up. Maybe because my mom thinks breakfast should be eaten at home, wearing pajamas, he automatically does the opposite.

Jane had torn off the corner of a sugar packet and was quietly dipping her finger in and then licking it. Dad was reading the Arts & Leisure section of the Sunday paper. Harry must have been asleep inside my pack, because he was very still.

I slid the saucer from under the creamer and

casually slipped it onto my lap. Jane was instantly on alert.

"Dad!" she said in her informative voice. "Billie . . ."

I eyeballed the sugar packet and gave her a warning squint.

"Dad!" I said as a diversionary tactic.

"Mmmmm?" He turned a page.

"Did you put anything in your hair? I mean, it looks like you used cement or something. It hasn't moved."

I gently shifted the saucer to the floor.

"Oh, no! You can tell? I tried something new." He was patting his head in a panic, looking in the mirror behind me, trying to ruffle up his hair.

I quickly poured the water from my glass into Harry's saucer.

"I think it looks nice, Daddy," said Jane. "You look like a man in a magazine."

Harry barked.

I jumped half out of my chair. It was the first time he'd made a noise. And even though it was just a little bitty baby bark, it was still a very doglike noise. I had completely forgotten about this particular problem.

Jane and Dad were staring at me.

"Woof," I barked, as best I could. Dad raised an eyebrow, and Jane looked under the table. She sat back up and wrinkled her nose at me.

"Meow?" I tried as I slipped a PuppySnack out of my pocket and dropped it by my sneaker.

Jane grinned. "R-R-Roar!" Now it was a game.

Dad glanced around at the other brunchers and glared at us.

"Can we save the animal noises for the park, girls?"

"Sure, Dad," I agreed. "I was just making conversation."

The food came. Jane and I both had waffles. It's kind of a test to see how many times we can ask for more syrup before my dad gets fed up.

I now know that Harry loves waffles. He stood up on his back legs, scratching my knees with his paws, begging for food.

I started to hum, to cover the panting. I felt like a grain elevator, passing chunks down to

him every twenty seconds. He ate half my breakfast, and nobody noticed. Except my stomach.

No offense to Dad, but he's not completely aware of his surroundings at all times. That might be why he's a great artist; he can create a beautiful idea in his mind while he's doing the dishes. Even though it sometimes feels like he's just not paying attention.

But I knew the real test of Harry's life would be my mother.

7 • It Followed Her to School One Day

The problem with staying at Dad's house, way up there on 104th Street, is that we had to get up when it was practically still dark to be at school on time. But having only one clothing option cut down Jane's preparations by about an hour, so that helped. Plus, the motherly concept of serving a nourishing breakfast is way too humdrum for Dad. We just ducked into Dunkin' Donuts on the way to the subway and picked up a few Munchkins for the long ride.

Of course, today I had the small extra problem of Harry. The morning routine was pretty much the same as yesterday, except that I only had to deal with pee and not poop. Dad was running out of toilet paper. And I didn't have any PuppySnack left.

"Oh, Harry," I said, making a cradle with my arms and burrowing my face into his fur. "I solemnly promise to get you more food as soon as I can."

He understood because he licked me.

Money. I was going to need more money than usual.

"Dad," I said on the train, "you forgot to give us our allowance. Saturday is allowance day."

"Your mother usually does allowance, doesn't she?" he asked.

"Yeah, but she forgot, and we were with you on Saturday."

Jane opened her big mouth. "But she gave—"

"That was last week, Jane," I said firmly. "You're mixed up."

"Okay," said Dad. "How much is it? You get five?"

"Uh-huh, and Jane gets three."

"Yeah, I get three, Daddy." She was a quick learner.

He pulled out his wallet and counted out the bills.

"Let me look after yours, Jane," I offered. "I have a pocket with a zipper."

She was about to say, "No way," but Dad agreed, and I was suddenly eight dollars richer. Very smooth, I thought proudly. Now I can feed my baby!

Outside the school was the usual crowd. Kids waiting till the last minute to go inside. A homeless man named Clifton, who always does the daily crossword puzzle leaning against the railing. A teenager walking by with about seven dogs on leads. A few mothers debating where they should go for coffee.

Dad kissed us good-bye.

"See you this afternoon, girls. Jane, you're going home with Katie, right? And Billie, I'll see you here at three-fifteen."

"Bye, Dad. Good luck with your presentation. I hope they like the new name stuff. Love you . . ."

Harry was starting to wriggle. I had to take Jane to her classroom, but I didn't want to take Harry, too, while he was so jumpy. Hubert, my savior, appeared at just the right moment.

"Hubert, do me a favor. Hold my backpack while I zoom up with Jane. Whatever you do, don't put it down!" I handed it over, grabbed Jane's hand, and turned to run.

"Hey! Good morning to you, too!" he called after me.

Jane wanted to show me her animal projects, so I had to coo over her beaver dam for a couple of minutes before I could gallop back to find Hubert.

He was lurking by the water fountain outside our class.

"Billie!" He has a knack of yelling and whispering at the same time. "You better tell me what's going on. There's something alive in here!"

He held my pack high in the air. Together we watched it jiggle and lurch as Harry tried to adjust to standing in midair.

"Yes, Billie," said a horribly familiar voice behind us. "Why don't you tell us what's in your backpack?"

My stomach jumped and fell.

It was Alyssa, my arch enemy.

8 • Close Call

She was staring up at my pack with wheels of evil spinning in her brain. If she found out about Harry, I would be dog food.

"Ha, ha, ha, good joke, Hubert!" I shouted. "You are really getting good at this magic illusion stuff!"

I distinctly heard a small, frightened bark.

I snatched my pack out of his hands and spun around to bump smack into Mr. Donaldson.

My face actually hit his chest. One of his

buttons pressed into my forehead. His shirt smelled like meadow-scented fabric softener. How embarrassing!

"Oh, my God!" I heard Hubert say softly, under Alyssa's squeaky cackle. Harry's paws were scratching the inside of my bag.

Mr. Donaldson just stood there looking down at me.

"How's your nose?" he asked in a nice voice.

"Okay," I mumbled. "Sorry."

"I'm wondering," he said in not quite so nice a voice, "why certain members of my class are out here hollering while the rest of them are sitting quietly at their desks?"

"We're coming, sir," I said, hugging my pack to my chest and slipping past him.

"Right away, sir," said Hubert, on my heels.

"Sir?" began Alyssa. "I think there's something you should know. . . ."

Lucky for me, Mr. Donaldson was not so interested in what Alyssa had to say.

"And there are countless things I think you should know, Alyssa," he said impatiently. "Find your seat. Now."

He started to talk about life within the walls of a medieval castle.

At my desk, I unzipped my pack and immediately had my face washed with a happy tongue.

Hubert, at the next-door quartet of desks, stared and wiggled his fingers in a panic. I couldn't understand. I shook my head and tried to pay attention to the teacher while I scratched Harry behind the ears.

Twelve seconds later, Emma passed me a note from Hubert:

> *Pieces of your face were disappearing.*
> *It looks OK now.*
> *What's going on?*

I touched my face with my fingertips, but it felt normal. I realized in a flash that anything in the dog's mouth would disappear. When I was invisible, anything I held in my hand disappeared, but for a dog it was clearly different. I would have to be careful not to get licked in public!

Hubert was waiting. Shifting my eyes to the

right, I noticed that Alyssa was waiting, too. She was watching us both with close attention.

The thing about Alyssa is this: She's not too good at schoolwork because she doesn't listen and she's dumb. She's not too good at friendship because she's bossy and mean and sneaky. But because she's such a sneaky rat, she's very good at sniffing out ratlike tendencies in others. Even if you're just a mouse wearing rat ears temporarily. So I had to watch out for her.

Pretending to be fascinated by Mr. Donaldson, I wrote Hubert a note on the corner of my worksheet and tore it off.

It's a dog.

I squeezed the paper into a teeny ball and waited for a clear shot. Completing a perfect arc, it landed on Hubert's desk.

He unfolded it, read it, and dropped it, open-mouthed, in alarm.

"Can anyone tell me what might happen first if a castle was under siege?" asked Mr. Donaldson.

Alyssa's hand flew into the air.

"Yes, Alyssa?"

"Billie just passed a note to Hubert, and she has something bad in her backpack."

Mr. Donaldson looked at me. His furry eyebrows add power to his glare. He looked at Hubert, and he looked at Alyssa. "And what does that have to do with life in the Middle Ages?"

"Well, nothing, sir, but she does."

"What do you have in your backpack, Billie?" Mr. Donaldson strolled in my direction, running his fingers across the desktops along the way. "Are you carrying drugs or firearms?"

"No, sir."

"Well, what then? Please share it with the class, whatever is causing the rumpus."

He leaned over me, and I held my breath.

Please don't bark, Harry, I was thinking. Please, please, please, don't bark.

Pretending to spread open the top flap, I groped inside for Harry's head. I stroked his neck with the slightest motion. Mr. D. could see my binder, and my history book and my bottle of water. And nothing else.

Mr. Donaldson patted my shoulder. "Thank

you, Billie. In the future, take out the books you need and keep the pack in your locker. Alyssa, a spy should be certain of her information before jeopardizing her reputation.

"This nonsense has put an end to the Middle Ages for today. Read chapter eleven in the text tonight.

"Put your things together, class, and make your way quietly down to the computer lab. Ms. Lobel is expecting you in five minutes."

9 • *Hubert Meets Harry*

Where are you going?" hissed Hubert as I headed down the wrong stairs for the computer lab.

"We have to make a detour," I hissed back.

"We? Billie, I don't like this." Hubert is such a worrywart, he could be a grandfather already.

As we passed the bathroom in the first-floor stairwell, I grabbed his arm.

"Quick, come in here!" I dragged him in and closed the door before he could open his fussy mouth.

"Billie, you are a bully. That should be your name. Billie the Bully, like a Viking. And another thing. What do you mean, 'It's a dog'?"

I opened my backpack and lifted Harry out. He gave a couple of excited yips and shook himself so that I had to put him down to avoid dropping him.

"Hubert," I announced, "allow me to introduce Harry. Harry, this is my best friend, Hubert, so be nice. Don't pee on his jeans or anything."

Hubert gasped. "Oh, Billie, don't tell me . . . You're kidding, right? Please say that I've gone cuckoo, because that would be *so* much better than what I think is going on here. . . ."

"I wanted you to meet him," I said, ignoring his tirade. Harry was licking my ankle. I lifted him into my arms and headed out into the hallway again. Hubert was tripping over himself, trying to keep up.

"What we need," I said, pausing beside the

Lost & Found box in the front hall, "is a leash."

I was hoping for a belt or a bag strap.

"What you need is a brain," muttered Hubert.

"I'm disappointed in you, Hubert. I especially wanted you to meet him," I said, digging with one hand among the abandoned sweatshirts and lone sneakers while Harry batted me with his paw.

"You're the only person I can tell, because you were there the first time. Jody's dog, Pepper, remember her? She had puppies, only my mom won't let me have one, so we had this idea and—"

"And it's a dumb idea, Billie. You have a dog that no one can see! What's the point? The whole point is to think your dog is the cutest dog and to teach him cute tricks and to go around looking at your cute dog all day."

"Oh, he's cute all right. He's the cutest. Hey!" I'd found the perfect thing.

"Look!" From the bottom, I pulled out a fluorescent pink skipping rope.

"Billie, I'm going to computer lab."

"Just come with me for one second," I insisted.

I coiled the rope around my wrist and carried Harry in my arms, making Hubert lug my pack.

In the library, I crouched down beside the shelf with domestic animal books, Dewey decimal number 636. My mother's substitute was a parent volunteer. She had her glasses about two inches away from a fat book called *Murder on Long Island*, so I figured we were safe.

I put Harry on the floor and got him to sit next to my knees. I plucked the *Encyclopedia of Dogs* from its place and started to flip through the pages.

"What are you doing?" demanded Hubert.

"Hold your horses. I'm going to show you what he looks like so you'll know I've got the cutest dog."

I flipped the pages back and forth, hunting for a picture that looked like Harry. Harry leaned against my thigh, panting as usual.

"See? Sort of like that."

Harry is a mutt with a large dose of terrier. I

showed Hubert the closest, cutest picture I could find.

" 'Personality,' " I read aloud, " 'courageous, merry, devoted, obedient.' See? Who could ask a dog for anything more?"

I pulled another book called *Puppy Care Guide for Children*.

"Here," I said, handing it to Hubert, "sign this out."

"Why me? I already have a book out. *All About Armor*."

"Hubert, just do it. I can't have it on record that I took out this book. My mother is the librarian, in case you don't remember."

"Very funny."

It was just plain bad luck that Ms. McPhee came in just then, trailed by a few of her students. She was our teacher last year, and she gets overexcited whenever she spots one of her "old" kids.

"Billie! Hubert! How nice to see you here! Are you doing some special research?"

"Er, um, yeah, sort of . . ." We mumbled a duet.

Suddenly Hubert lurched to one side and did a funny, leaning dance, trying to shake his left foot. I noticed that his shoelaces were disappearing.

"What are you working on this year?" asked Ms. McPhee, oblivious to Hubert's discomfort.

"Oh, it's so interesting," I jumped in, trying to shield Hubert from close inspection. "We're learning about the Middle Ages and how they never brushed their teeth or washed their hair or anything."

Hubert was swaying behind me.

"Well." Ms. McPhee nodded. "I won't keep you. We have our own work to do, don't we, kids?" She beamed at her group, and they moved off to the index files.

Hubert had just managed to tug himself free when Harry made a low, ominous growl. I'd heard it only once before, but already I knew what it meant.

"Hubert!" I panicked. "Grab the tissue box and follow me!" I picked up Harry, almost by the scruff of the neck, and ran with him, dangling, up the back stairs and into the courtyard.

Then I dropped him, not too gently, onto the ground.

"Okay," I said, "it's safe now. You can poop out here."

"Billie, that's completely disgusting," said Hubert.

But Harry performed his duty, and we waited for it to appear, and I cleaned it up and tossed it into the garbage can. I think Hubert was a little bit impressed.

Until the door swung open and our class came bursting out with hollers of freedom, and Hubert realized that it was recess time and he'd just cut computer class for the first time in his life.

10 • Recess

Recess!

We went behind the bike racks where no one else was playing. Most of the kids went straight to the basketball court. Alyssa was whispering with Megan and Tonya in the corner. Nobody paid attention to us.

Hubert picked up a tennis ball from the equipment bin and rolled it along the ground. After a second, it skittered off course and then completely disappeared.

"Good dog!" I whispered. "Now, let's see if you have any retriever in you. Bring back the ball." I pointed sternly and waited with my hand out. Harry nudged me, not dropping the ball, but wanting me to wrestle him for it.

"Oh, Hubert, I wish you could see him. You would fall in love."

"With a dog?"

I rolled the ball again and Harry brought it back. This time he put it down right at my feet. It was getting soggy, like a big, slimy lemon.

"Throw it," Hubert suggested. "Make it harder."

I threw it up above our heads and as it came down, it vanished in midair. Harry was jumping for it!

"What a clever boy you are!" I said when he brought the ball back. My voice sounded like a proud nanny.

"You're such a smart boy."

I tossed the ball long. We could hear his nails clicking faintly on the asphalt as he raced to be in position.

"I admit, this is kind of cool." Hubert laughed as we watched Harry fetch, over and over again.

Until Harry started to bark. He was so excited, he just started to bark and wouldn't stop, the way a little kid gets the giggles.

I threw the ball, thinking he'd be quiet with his mouth full, but he kept on barking.

"Billie, don't throw the ball again," Hubert warned. "We've got company."

David, chasing a stray basketball, was lingering, and his teammates were closing in. Alyssa, noticing a crowd gathering, was, of course, coming over, too.

Harry kept barking. And then Hubert did the bravest thing he's ever done. Especially when

you consider that for Hubert, "brave" is putting his hand up in class.

Hubert started to bark. And he barked just like Harry, same pitch, same rhythm. Harry must have been so surprised that he stopped immediately, probably sniffing around for the other dog.

By this time, Mr. Donaldson was there, too. Everybody in the class was there, and Hubert just kept on barking, glaring at me till he was cross-eyed, his face turning bright pink.

Finally he stopped for breath. He ducked his head down so he wouldn't have to look at anyone, but the whole crowd began to applaud.

"That was pretty impressive, Hubert," said Mr. Donaldson. "Would you like to explain your little concert?"

"Oh, I can," I interrupted, assuming that Hubert would be catatonic for a couple of hours after such a public display. "We're working on an idea for the medieval pageant."

"Well, I can't wait to hear it," said Mr. D., with teacherly enthusiasm. I thought Hubert might fall over with the strain of keeping his head lowered out of eye-contact range.

"But for now, recess is over."

Everyone groaned and headed slowly for the door.

"Group A, you've got Spanish. Group B, you've got shop. Let's go, people. . . ." Mr. Donaldson led the way.

"Shall I kill you now, or later?" Hubert was sweating and still faintly scarlet.

"Hubert, you were beyond brilliant." He gave a little bow. "But," I added urgently, "we don't have time to dwell on your future career as a canine impressionist. Harry has disappeared!"

11 • *Second Thoughts*

May I remind you, Billie, that Harry has never been anything *but* disappeared as far as I'm concerned?"

"No, I mean, really! He's not here anymore! See, the ball is right over there, against the wall, and Harry is nowhere."

"Oh, sh-sh-sugar cube!" Hubert swore. "Sh-sh-shoulder!"

"Hey, guys!" Sarah called from the doorway. "C'mon!"

"Go ahead!" I said. "We'll be right there." Sarah waved, and the door swung shut behind her.

"Harry!" I called softly. "Here, boy! Harry!"

Hubert whistled and bounced the ball as a temptation.

There was deadly silence. I mean, except for the traffic on the other side of the wall, and a jackhammer in the alley, and a siren a couple of blocks away, and the sound of the kindergarten singing through an open window. There was dog silence. There was no panting.

I felt a chill race up my spine and settle in across my shoulders. This must be what it's like when a mother turns around in the supermarket and her kid is gone.

"Harry? Please? Harry?"

I started in one direction around the perimeter of the yard, and Hubert went the other way. I whistled, I said his name, I waved my arms and snapped my fingers and clucked my tongue.

Was he just hiding out? Chasing his tail? Or had he gone inside with the rest of the class? Where was my heart's delight?

And then, as Hubert bounced the ball, it disappeared!

"Harry!" We both screamed with joy and ran toward him. I stepped on his paw, and he yowled. The ball dropped and rolled.

I picked him up and rubbed my face in his neck. I inhaled his delicious doggy smell and kissed his silky ears. It was the happiest moment of my whole life so far. Even Hubert leaned over to pat his back.

"Good to see you, little buddy," he said. "I mean, good to have you back. You gave us a scare."

And then, in a different voice altogether, he added, "Billie, we already missed computer lab. We've got to go to Spanish."

I was fiddling with tying the skipping rope around Harry's neck. He kept ducking his head, trying to sneak away. I decided to leave it till later. I couldn't go around cuddling a skipping rope all day anyway.

"Mr. D. always has to flirt with Ms. Picayo for at least ten minutes. We won't be late."

"What are you going to do with Harry all day? This is getting ridiculous!"

"I don't know what else to do."

"Well, you can't keep him invisible like this. This is the worst. We lost him for two minutes inside a playground, and it was scary. Think about if that happened on the street? He'd go in the road and be puppy mush in two seconds!"

What a horrible thought. The chill went right through me this time, leaving my blood frozen. I wondered whether death would make him reappear. Then I closed my eyes to stop thinking about that.

"You're right, Hubert," I admitted, "I haven't been very responsible. . . . He needs a collar so we can keep track of him."

"A collar? Billie, he needs a life!"

"Well, what should we do?"

"How should I know? We should go to Spanish before we get expelled."

I buttoned my sweater around Harry so that he could ride on my chest with his face peeking out.

"Maybe he'll fall asleep after all that exercise," I said as he snuggled against me. "I guess at lunchtime we better call Jody and ask her for help."

I knew in my heart that meant giving him back, but I couldn't say those words out loud.

12 • *In a Muddle*

Harry slept through Spanish, as did most of the class.

And he slept through most of reading time. When I felt him waking up, I asked if I could go to the bathroom, and I gave him a long drink of water at the sink. I've heard that lots of dogs drink out of toilets, but Harry was so little, I was afraid he might fall in.

The door opened so quickly, it hit me in the back.

"Oh, sorry," said Sarah. "Mr. Donaldson wanted me to check if you were okay, 'cause you were taking so long."

"I'm fine," I said, quickly putting my own hands under the stream of water that Harry was trying to drink from.

"Or, uh, at least, well, actually . . ."

I changed my mind. "I'm not feeling great, actually. I think I'm going to the nurse's office to lie down for a few minutes. Maybe this, um, dizziness, will pass. Could you tell Mr. D.?"

"Sure," said Sarah. "I hope you feel better. It's tacos for lunch." The door slammed behind her.

"You might like tacos, puppy boy," I told Harry. "But we have to make a phone call first."

The problem with the phone booth is that it's directly opposite from Ms. Shephard. She's the receptionist who has a teeny office right inside the front door, and she thinks she's paid to know everything about anybody's business.

I ignored her snoopy smile and shut the door.

I dialed Jody's number. After four rings, I

was thinking, *Duh, she's at school,* when someone answered with a hello that covered half a
keyboard.

"Hello?" You could never tell from reading
the word how many notes were involved. It
must be Jody's mother.

"Uh, yes, hello? I need to speak with Jody, I
mean, I know she's at school, but I need to give
her a message."

"I can take a message for you, dear." She was
practically singing. "But she won't be home
tonight. Jody is participating in a little state science fair at Putter College. The Putter College
Young Inventors Competition. The final demon-
strations are taking place this evening—"

"But it's very important that I speak with
her today!"

"Well, I suppose you could leave a message at
the Bingham School. I don't think the bus is
leaving until after class time. Who is this, dear?"

"Thank you," I said. And I hung up. I was
sweating. Harry was gnawing on something that
I couldn't see. I carefully shifted my feet so I
wouldn't step on him.

This news was terrible. It was disastrous, horrible, calamitous. There weren't enough words to say how completely awful this was.

I felt Harry's tail thwacking against my ankle. I knelt down to pet him with tears prickling my eyes.

"Come on, Harry," I said, buttoning him into my sweater again. "We have to consult with Hubert."

I got back to class just as the lunch bell rang.

"How are you feeling, Billie?" asked Mr. Donaldson from the doorway as I grabbed Hubert.

"Much better, thanks."

"So what really happened?" asked Hubert on the way to the cafeteria.

"There's bad news, and there's worse news," I told him.

Alyssa and Megan joined the line behind us, balancing their trays on their heads.

"Well, well, well, if it isn't the little lovebirds!" exclaimed Alyssa in her shrieky voice. "Let's just sit at the next table and get all warm and fuzzy. . . ."

So much for my conversation with Hubert. I

fed most of my taco to Harry by spilling it down my front. He was still buttoned into my sweater and very happy to get room service.

Sixth-graders have the outstanding privilege of being allowed to leave school grounds without a pass. This means that we tend to exit in a herd right after lunch, when we are the most hungry, and go to the deli down the block.

I paused on the front steps of the school, making Hubert stay back while I tied the skipping rope around Harry's neck and let it trail down from my backpack in a way that looked casual but was pretty secure.

"When was the last time you played with a skipping rope, Billie?" asked Hubert, with a sneer for my plan.

I socked him on the arm.

"About three years ago," I admitted. "Anyway, I tried to call Jody."

I filled him in while we caught up with the others.

"You just love trouble, don't you?" he asked. "And it loves you."

"I'm going to wait out here," I told him when

we got to the store. "See the sign? No Dogs Allowed."

He looked at me and shook his head before he went grumbling inside.

Less than a minute later, Harry gave such a tug on the rope that I was jerked around sideways. A teenager boy was coming our way holding a bundle of leashes connected to a pack of dogs.

Harry was so excited to see a party of his own kind that he yelped and pulled hard enough that the skipping rope came undone from my pack. It slithered along the sidewalk, following what must be a fast-running Harry.

13 • A Knight with No Armor

The boy stared, first at the rope and then at me. His dogs were barking a chorus of greetings, and their master couldn't figure out why.

He had a dalmatian and a golden Lab and a

sheepdog and two rottweilers. Five huge dogs, all sniffing and barking and prancing in a tizzy over my little Harry.

"Yo!" said the boy.

He was about seventeen maybe. He was wearing his baseball hat backward, and his skin was the color of fudge brownies. Just like a million other teenagers in New York City, his shoelaces were untied.

"Yo!" I tried to sound like it wasn't the first time I'd ever said it.

"Whassup?" the boy asked. It took me a second to realize he'd said "What's up?" And I was working on my answer when he continued.

"Whaddya got there?"

We watched together as the skipping rope became more and more ensnarled with the leashes of his charges, creating a spaghetti-like mess of leather and nylon and fluorescent pink plastic.

"Are all those yours?" I asked.

"Nah. I'm a dog walker. It's my job. I love dogs. But I gotta admit, I never saw one like yours before." He turned his brown eyes on me and showered me with such a twinkling smile that I knew instantly I could trust him.

"Listen," I said, "maybe you can help me. I . . . I . . . I have this problem. My dog got invisible."

"I can see that."

"And I need to make him reappear, but it's really hard for him to be at school, and I'm having trouble finding . . ."

The boy knelt down and felt for Harry in the muddle of dogs.

"Hey," he said gently, "I'm cool. I'll take your dog for the afternoon. He seems to get along with my gang. You do what you have to do."

"Can you come back at three-fifteen when we get out?" I pleaded.

The door of the deli swung open, and Hubert came out with a coconut Frozfruit in his mouth. Charley and Alyssa were on his tail. Half the sixth grade were crowding out behind them.

They all stopped dead at the sight of the boy and me.

"What's his name?" I was being asked a question.

"His name is Harry," I whispered.

"Harry? I like it. I'm Sam, by the way."

"Hi, Sam," I said, feeling relieved and terrified at the same time. "I'm Billie. I'm, um, not supposed to, you know—"

He grinned. "Talk to strangers? Or have an invisible puppy? Which is worse?"

I grinned back.

"I'll catch you at three-fifteen, Shortie."

He winked and leaned over to straighten out the leashes wrapped around his legs, clicking his tongue and murmuring to the dogs. I kept watching until he sauntered off down the block, saluting me without looking back.

"Billie!" Alyssa's screech broke my trance. "You were talking to that . . . that . . . drug dealer!"

"He's not a drug dealer, you idiot," I scoffed.

"Only drug dealers have five dogs for protection," she insisted. "You are really begging for trouble."

She clattered off toward school on her stupid new platform shoes from Delia's.

"The guy was looking for Morton Street," I said to the other kids. "Not selling heroin."

Hubert pulled on my arm as we all headed back to school.

"You let him take Harry? A total stranger? Have you completely lost your brain?"

"He's just going to dog-sit for the afternoon. First, you were itching about having him in class, and now you're twitching that I came up with a better solution."

"We'll see," he said, threatening doom.

"Come on," I said as we went inside. "I still have to get in touch with Jody. I'm going to have to call her school."

Hubert balanced the phone book on his knees while I looked up Bingham School. I'd never even heard of it. It sounded snooty and English. No wonder Jody hated it. I dialed the number. A snooty person with an English accent answered.

"Bingham. May I help you?"

"Yes," I said, lowering my voice and trying to make it boom a little. "Yes, I need to speak to one of your students on an urgent matter. Could you contact Jody Greengard, please?"

"I can take your number and have her call you back at the class interval."

"No, no, that won't do," I said firmly, and sounding very mature. "I will wait on the line for you to locate her. This is of the utmost urgency!"

Hubert snorted. I kicked his shin. I was delighted with myself. Where were these words coming from? I could hear the secretary complaining to someone, but she went off to do my bidding.

I had to add two extra nickels to the phone while I waited, but finally I heard Jody's voice, breathless and wary.

"Hello? Hello?"

"Jody, it's me, Billie, I'm sorry, but I had to talk to you."

"Oh, my God, I thought someone had died," said Jody, laughing and whispering. "Thanks for getting me out of music. We should do this more often. Actually, I can't really talk here. Let me call you right back on my cell phone. What's the number?"

I read her the numbers written on the front of the pay phone.

"I'll call you right back, as soon as I get to the bathroom," promised Jody.

Those three minutes felt like twenty-three minutes. The bell ending the lunch break sounded. Hubert scuttled back to class, armed with a story about gum on my sneaker to cover my lateness.

Alone, I suddenly panicked, thinking Harry should be with me. I'd had his tail or his tongue or his warmth next to me all day. His panting had been as steady as a heartbeat. Now I felt I'd lost something.

When the phone finally rang, it echoed in the booth like a saucepan lid falling down stairs. I snatched the receiver with both hands.

"What's up?" Jody asked without wasting time on a hello. "How's Harry? Pepper misses him so much, you wouldn't believe it. The last two nights she keeps nudging the other puppies, like she's counting them, and then she trots all over the house, looking for Harry. How is he?"

"Oh, I feel so bad for Pepper. Harry's okay, except it's not working out very well." I told her about Harry's day at school, and about the choked and chilling feeling I had when he got lost in the playground.

"Where is he now?"

I told her about Sam.

"He sounds totally cute," said Jody.

"Well, I guess he is," I said. "But that's not the point. It's just not, uh, responsible for Harry to live this way. It's not fair. We have to make him reappear, and then I have to give him back to you." I swallowed so I wouldn't cry. "I'm sorry. I know he needs a home."

"Billie, I'm really impressed with you. You're completely right about all of this. Have you got a pencil?" Her voice dropped low. "Someone just came into the next stall."

We waited for the flush before Jody went on. "The competition is tonight, so there's nothing I can do today. Tomorrow is a half day, in honor of our founder, the great Bernice Bingham." She made a gagging noise.

"So, I could come down at the end of morning classes to pick him up. I'm sorry. I know you really want him. I'll give you the recipe for the bath. You'll have to do it yourself. Get Hubert to help you. I'll give you my cell phone number, just in case. Have you got a piece of paper? Okay, listen . . ."

She recited a list of ingredients, and I wrote them down on the back page of the phone book.

"That's it," she said. "I gotta go. Good luck, okay?"

She hung up. I could hear my heart. I raced back to class, where they were splitting up into groups for poetry study. I attached myself to Hubert and talked fast.

"I called Jody. She gave me the recipe. Most of it is easy stuff to get, like water and talcum powder and dog biscuits. Then there's the chewed-up-gum juice."

Hubert cracked the first smile I'd seen all day.

"I remember the last time we had to do this," he whispered, pretending to study the verse in front of him. "I must have chewed about twelve packs of gum in one day."

"In one hour," I told him proudly. "You were the best. We collected gobs of it in paper cups. But that's the easy part. We also have to get tubers of lilyturf and make teas from chrysanthemum flowers and powdered goat horn. How the heck are we going to do that?"

Now Hubert's smile turned big and pearly enough to make him a poster boy for Dentists of America.

"No problem," he said happily. "Call your dad and ask if you can come over to my place after school. I know exactly where to find what we need."

14 • Chinatown

When we came out of the building at three-fifteen, Sam was waiting at the foot of the steps. He had only the sheepdog and the dalmatian, along with Harry's pink lead. He was being eyed suspiciously by the assistant principal who oversees the departures, but as soon as Sam smiled, even that iceberg melted.

Making the handover was a delicate operation, with so many people all around us, but Hubert and I had prepared in advance.

Hubert greeted his mother and begged her to get us a drink from the deli. I signaled Sam to follow us, and while we waited outside the store for Hubert's mom, Sam passed me Harry, away from the prying onlookers at school.

"Yo!" I said. "Thanks a million. I mean it."

"Hey," said Sam, "this is a mighty puppy. Same time tomorrow?"

"Well, I don't know," I faltered. "I might not have him anymore . . . but . . ."

"I'll come by anyway, just to check." He flashed another radiant smile. "See ya, Shortie."

I nodded, hoping he knew how grateful I was. He strolled away, just as our drinks arrived.

I love going to Hubert's house. It's an apartment, just big enough for his parents and him, on the corner of Canal Street and Mulberry, right in the heart of Chinatown.

Canal Street is bursting with busyness. The sidewalk is crowded with market stalls selling everything from huge fish with their heads on, to eels to bok choy to lemongrass, and lots of other things that Americans don't usually eat. There are bins and bins of dried—well, dried things, that I have no idea what they are. All the signs are in Chinese. It all gets weighed on old-fashioned scales and packaged in little red bags. It seems like a different country.

"I pick up few things for supper," said Hubert's mom at the entrance of his building. "You want come?"

She talks in shorthand, as if using all those little connecting words is just another sign of American wastefulness.

"Nah," said Hubert. "We'll see you upstairs, Mama."

"You have key?"

He showed it to her. She kissed him and went off down the street, swallowed up by the crowd in seconds.

I turned to go inside. Hubert pulled me back out to the sidewalk.

"Come on, Billie. This is our chance. Follow me."

I wasn't used to Hubert being the leader, but since we were on his territory, it seemed right.

"Wait a sec," I said. I took Harry out of my pack and put the skipping rope around his neck. He might as well get some exercise.

We stepped into the flow of people and trotted along, past food stalls and guys selling fake designer watches and handbags and glittery jewelry and sunglasses.

Harry was tugging this way and that, trying to smell everything. We turned off Canal onto a twisty side street, full of restaurants and blinking dragons on lit-up signs.

Hubert stopped suddenly beside a window painted with lots of Chinese characters and then in English:

LIN HOP SISTERS
HERBAL SPECIALISTS

"This is it," Hubert said with satisfaction. "They'll have everything, I'm sure of it."

Inside was a long glass counter displaying twisted roots and dry, gnarly twigs. Baskets holding pods and seeds and brown petals. Huge mushrooms and anthills of different-colored powders.

It's kind of amazing how, in New York, a person can find a brand-new something to look at every day.

The wall behind the counter was made of wooden drawers. From the ceiling all the way down were rows of drawers, each about the size of a dictionary. In a slot above each handle was a card with a character, I guess saying what was inside. All I could think was how tidy my room would be if I had all those places to put stuff in.

There were two women wearing white doctor jackets behind the counter. I realized they were twin pharmacists.

They were wearing pins printed with their names, Lin Lee and Lin Sue. Lin Lee said something to Hubert in Chinese. I haven't heard Hubert speak Chinese very often—he always uses English in front of me, even with his mom.

But, even in another language, I could tell he was feeling shy. I pulled out the list for him to explain what we needed, and the woman looked curious and surprised. Her voice was like chimes; Hubert's was softer, like a flute. I felt as if I were listening to a concert.

Lin Lee opened a drawer and pulled out a fistful of chrysanthemum petals, looking brown and wilted, like they do a week after Mother's Day. Then a little pile of what looked like overgrown rice. That was the tubers of lilyturf. The powdered goat horn came in a tiny brown bottle.

She wrote down what I figured were the prices on a paper bag as she went along, but I couldn't read them. I nervously fingered the eight dollars my dad had given me that morning.

She gave the price to Hubert in Chinese, and he translated for me.

"Five dollars and eighty-two cents," he said. "Do you have enough?"

I handed her six one-dollar bills and took the lumpy bag in exchange. She gave me eighteen cents and wished us "Happy Luck" in English.

Outside it was getting darker already.

"We have to get dog food," I reminded Hubert. "Harry hasn't eaten since breakfast. The book says he has to eat at least three times a day, maybe four."

We stopped at a dim, poky grocery store on the corner and bought two tins of food and the smallest box of dog biscuits.

At Hubert's house, I used the can opener on the Power Puppy Beef with Cheddar Surprise. It was disgustingly slimy and smelled like barf. I dumped it onto a saucer and put the dish on the floor. The muck disappeared as Harry slurped and chomped his way through it.

At my house, snacks are always apples or carrots or something bursting with nutrients. Hubert is allowed to have stuff like Ring Ding Juniors and Chips Ahoy, as long as he drinks milk. His mom is a big believer in milk. I've learned that every grown-up has at least one area of being peculiar.

So we had milk and Devil Dogs at the kitchen table with our feet up on the bathtub. Their bathtub is in the kitchen because that's the way they built these little apartments back then, with all the plumbing together. He says when he was a baby, his mom could wash his hair with one hand and stir supper with the other. Now, of course, he waits for her to be in the living room.

"We better get down to business," said Hubert, licking the chocolate off his fingers. "We have to reappear a dog, plus do a ton of homework."

We could hear Harry running back and forth in the living room, his paws thudding on the carpet and then skittering off onto the floor.

I pulled out the recipe for Jody's potion.

"Water," I read. "About two gallons, she said."

"Not a problem," said Hubert. "As you can see, we do have modern plumbing."

"Dog biscuits."

"Check."

"Baby powder."

"Uh, probably." Hubert leaned over and opened a little cupboard under the end of the bathtub. There was shampoo and conditioner and something green, and baby powder.

"Check," said Hubert. "My dad uses it on his feet, between his toes."

"I don't need to know that, Hubert." I looked back at my notes.

"Oh, no!" I smacked my forehead, like a cartoon character. "How could we be so stupid?"

"What?" asked Hubert.

"We forgot the gum!!!"

Hubert moaned and put his face in his hands.

"We have to have gum!" I wailed. "You have to go get it right now!"

I pushed him up on his feet. He was pulling on his jacket when the buzzer rang.

"Who is it?" Hubert said into the intercom.

"It's Billie's dad," came the crackling reply.

15 · *At Home*

It would be Harry's first night in his new home. Except it wasn't going to be his home, so it was also his last night. How could I ever have imagined that I could keep a dog a secret? It was kind of thrilling to have a secret from Mom and

Jane, but I was exhausted after only two days. I guess I hadn't realized that a dog is a whole person who can't live happily in hiding.

I'd had four minutes from the time my father buzzed till he climbed the stairs to the fourth floor. I grabbed the ingredients together and shoveled them into a plastic bag from under Hubert's sink. I stopped Harry from chewing the kitchen table leg and put him in my pack, which was getting crowded, by the way. And I issued orders to Hubert, who was standing like a tree in the Petrified Forest.

"Get the gum. Do you have any money?" He nodded.

"Good. Get the gum. Chew like crazy all through homework and save the globs, still with flavor, remember? Save them in a Ziploc bag. Do you have Ziploc bags?"

He nodded.

"And bring it to school tomorrow. We'll have to do it at school, first thing. Oh, my God, this means I have to have him at home tonight! Good luck, and make sure you chew enough."

There was a knock.

"Oh, hi, Dad!"

We had to pick up Jane from her friend Katie's house on the way home to our loft on Broadway. When we got in, Dad stood for a minute in the doorway, looking around. Then he put down his overnight bag next to the sofa.

"It's okay if you sleep in your old bed, Dad," I said quietly.

"I don't think so," he said. "I'll be fine out here."

"I'm hungry," moaned Jane. She doesn't even remember when Dad used lived there, so she didn't care where he slept.

"Uh, just give me a minute, sweetie," said Dad. "I have to find my way around again."

I quick put my pack in my room and released Harry.

"Stay here," I whispered. "I'll be right back."

I got Jane a bowl of Kix while Dad unpacked the groceries he'd brought for supper. Once Jane was chewing away at the table, I made my move. I said I wasn't hungry and that I had loads of homework, and please leave me alone.

I should explain that our loft used to be a factory in the olden days. Now it's like an apartment, except with no real walls and no privacy. The only doors are on the bathroom and my mom's room. Everything else is open. Jane and I live together, hidden from the rest of the space by a half wall as high as my dad's head.

So I went to my room, but it's not like I was alone or anything. It took four seconds to find Harry. He was jumping around and sniffing everywhere.

I could sort of follow his path, as the Lego tower wobbled, and the revolver from Clue skidded off the board, and the middle of Jane's bed bounced, and my new fleece slipper disappeared completely until I ran over and got it away from him. I scolded him and took him back to my desk.

I unpacked my bag, retrieving the squished homework folder and the water bottle from the bottom. Harry lay across my knees like an old lady's lap rug, panting and adjusting his paws.

I rubbed his head while I tackled my first worksheet. We had to find definitions for big words from the text we'd read in class.

Indignant. That was an easy one, since I feel it ten times a day. I kept stroking Harry while I flipped the pages of the dictionary for the official meaning: *angry at something unworthy, unjust, or mean.*

Yearning. Oh, dear. *A longing or desire; desire earnestly.* I was overcome suddenly with an earnest desire to see Harry. I imagined him in the last position I'd actually seen him, with his paws folded over his nose. I yearned for him.

I pulled up the stopper on my water bottle and had a drink. Harry's panting became louder, and I could feel those oversize paws trying to stand up on my knees. I tipped the bottle and squirted a dribble of water in the general direction of his mouth so that he'd get the idea. I guess I was thinking he could suck it like a baby, but instead, he chewed on the end.

I held the bottle up higher and squirted again. This time, he opened his mouth and started to drink as I released a tiny stream. It dropped through the air and disappeared into his mouth.

"What a clever boy you are," I said, nuzzling his ear. "I should take you on TV. We could get rich."

"How did you do that?" Jane's whisper made me jump nearly out of my jeans. "Will you show me that magic trick?"

16 • The Sisters' Club

Harry, still thirsty, barked once.

Jane stared at me, and I watched the clues fall into place in her ever-busy brain.

"You took Jody's puppy and made him imaginary. Didn't you?"

Her face was amazed and delighted. She had figured out the truth because it didn't occur to her that it was impossible to have an invisible dog. I could have opened a drawer and introduced her to the Tooth Fairy and she would say, "Nice to meet you."

"What's his name? Do you still call him Boy?"

"His name is Harry."

"Hairy? Yuck. I don't like that."

"Too bad. He's my dog and don't ever forget it."

"Does Daddy know?"

Uh-oh. Blabbermouth alert.

"Jane, you cannot say one word. I promise you, I'll give you anything you want, except my Anne of Green Gables T-shirt. This is top secret. A special, um, Sisters' Club secret! I'll let him sleep on your bed for one whole hour, but you can't tell Dad, or Mom either."

Jane's eyes were flickering. I could see her calculating the extent of her power. Luckily a six-year-old doesn't have the same range of vision that I have.

"He has to sleep on my bed all night, plus you have to give me your face paints that you got from Uncle John."

"He can sleep on your bed until you go to sleep, how about? And—"

"And I get your face paints."

"Okay, you drive a hard bargain," I agreed. She fell for that trick without any trouble. The face paints were stupid; they had Pocahontas on the lid. I was going to give them to her anyway.

"Can we dress him up? In Nonnie's clothes?" Nonnie was her doll.

"No! He's a dog! He's dignified!"

Jane came bounding forward, ready to play. Harry jumped off my lap and skittered away across the room, knocking over the Lego tower and ending up somewhere under the computer table.

"Jane! You ninny! You scared him!"

"I was only trying—"

"You are such an idiot! You—" I didn't have time to finish. Harry must have barreled out from under the table full speed because Jane suddenly fell backward with her arms flapping in the air. She was so surprised, her mouth looked like a doughnut. I burst out laughing, and then she did, too, even though she got up rubbing her bottom.

The next thing we knew, Harry was scampering out of our room and clattering his nails across the wooden floor of the living area.

We raced after him, trying to reach him before he got as far as the kitchen. I jumped ahead of where we thought he might be. The rag rug slid magically toward me like a flying carpet and then stopped dead as we heard his nails again, clacking under the dining table. He was foraging for food and did a better job than the vacuum cleaner. Crumbs and Cheerios vanished into thin air. Jane scraped a chair on the floor, moving it out of the way for better access. The noise must have scared him because he thudded over my sneaker in his move toward the kitchen.

Dad had the portable phone tucked against his ear as he poked through the refrigerator.

"Hey!" He hopped forward as if he'd been bumped from behind, knocking his head into the milk carton. The carton jumped from the shelf and began to leak through the folded top, all over Dad's loafers.

I dove to the floor, ready to take the blame for Harry. Jane threw a sponge from the sink that hit my head, as furry feet scrambled across my arm. My father was still talking, using the most tense, polite voice I ever heard. He swatted me away and shushed us, pointing to the phone.

Harry dodged me and went tearing back to our end of the loft, with his panting gathering steam. We galloped behind.

Then he barked. He liked this game. He barked again.

I had no choice. I followed Hubert's example and set to howling, like a pack of huskies dragging a sled across the tundra.

"Hey, you even had him in the restaurant with Daddy, didn't you?" Jane giggled.

"Turn down the volume, please, Billie," my father called, his voice barely containing his fury. "I'm on the phone with work."

Jane started to bark, too, adding little snarls and nearly choking with laughter at the same time.

"Girls! I'm trying to concentrate!" Suddenly, Dad was there, standing in front of us, tapping the phone against his palm. Harry wasn't stopping, so we couldn't either.

"Do you mind telling me just what the heck is going on?" my father demanded. "I had to tell my client I'd call him back."

I pressed my thumb, in a reminderly kind of way, between Jane's shoulder blades, and kept barking.

"Well, Daddy, woof," said Jane, "We, woof, have a new Sisters' Club, woof, and to join it, woof, we have to bark for five minutes without stopping, woof, woof."

My father shook his head in despair, plugged his ears, and walked back to the kitchen.

I knew Harry wouldn't stop unless we stopped, but we couldn't stop unless he did. It was kind of a never-ending circle. I crawled around on the floor until I found him. I carried him to Jane's lower bunk, pressing his face into my chest. The barking subsided, and the heavy panting took over. Finally, we had quiet. Jane and I stroked his back until he fell asleep.

The phone rang.

"Billie! Get the phone!" my father yelled.

"Why can't you?" I yelled back, making Harry twitch and startle.

"Sssh!" whispered Jane.

The phone rang again.

I slid off the bed and went to the kitchen.

"You're standing right there!" I complained. "Why do I have to get up?"

The phone rang again.

"It's not my phone," said my father, shrugging. "It feels weird."

I picked it up.

"Hello?"

"Hi, honey, it's Mom."

"Oh, hi, Mom."

"See?" said Dad.

17 • *Mommy, Phone Home*

I want to talk to Mommy!" Jane tried to shout in a whisper as she hurtled toward me. "Let me talk to Mommy!" She grabbed at the receiver.

I tortured her for two seconds, holding it above her head. Then I gave in, before she collapsed with yearning.

"Hi, Mommy," she said in her most annoying baby voice. How could she be so funny and big-kid one moment and such a baby brat the next?

I looked at Dad and rolled my eyes.

"I miss you, Mommy. Did you get me some bookmarks at the conference?" Jane smiled up at me and nodded, as if I cared.

"Uh-huh," she said. "Uh-huh."

"The word is 'yes,' " I hissed.

"Okay, Mommy." She started to pass me the phone and then remembered something.

"Oh!" she added, smirking at me. "I know something you don't know—"

"My turn!" I snatched the phone out of her hand. "Hi, Mom. How's the conference going?"

"Oh, it's great. Lots of wonderful new books this season. Listen, Jane seems to be missing me. Could you make an extra effort to be a backup mommy while I'm gone?"

"Dad's here. He's her father."

"It's not the same thing."

"You should give him a chance, Mom."

There was a beat of silence and then her perky voice.

"How are things there? Any news?"

Oh, just an invisible puppy.

"Not really. I mean, there is something, sort of, that I should maybe, I don't know, talk over with you, but it can wait."

"Is it a scary thing? Or important? I have time to listen now, honey."

"Uh, no, nothing special, it can wait."

"Well, okay. Moms miss kids, too, you know."

A thought of Pepper flashed through my mind.

"Remember, honey, I love you every minute, every day."

She always says that. Always. But this was the first time that I completely knew what she meant. I'd been loving Harry every minute since he first climbed out of Jody's bag. I surprised her with an answer.

"I love you, too, Mom."

"Thank you, honey." She cleared her throat. "Well, I'll be back tomorrow, in time to see your medieval pageant. How's it going with your father?"

I hate it when she calls him that.

"Are you having a pizza?"

"No, Mom, he's actually cooking."

I could see Dad shake his head in disbelief that she would think otherwise.

"Really? That's great. Let me talk to him for a second. Bye, now."

I lingered, hoping to hear their conversation, but Dad just mumbled a few words and then hung up. He went back to cooking without glancing at me.

"Janie," he said, "come and be my special helper, okay? I'll teach you to use the can opener."

Big step in father-daughter bonding, I thought.

I went to make sure Harry was still napping. Jane had covered him with Nonnie's blanket, which was rising and falling with his every breath.

I had a job to do. While Hubert was chewing gum over at his house, I had to concoct "teas" out of powdered goat horn and chrysanthemum petals.

Toting the brown paper bag from Lin Hop Sisters, and two old Sippy-Cups with snap-on lids, I went to the bathroom. I was grateful for the garlic that Dad was sautéing. Chrysanthemums, mixed with a little hot water and set to soaking, sure let off a dose of bad smell.

Harry was not on the bed when I got back. The doll's quilt was on the floor. My heart skipped a couple of beats. Swallowing panic, I stood still and listened. Sure enough, a gnawing noise was coming from under Jane's bed, where Harry was trying to remove the doll shoes that Jane had put on his feet while I was on the phone.

If only I could keep him. But maybe my mother was right. Maybe I just wasn't ready to look after someone else without messing up.

18 • *Middle Age Madness*

I'm not sure if I slept in between nightmares, but I don't think so. I had a dream about rolling onto Harry and squishing him to death, I had a dream about Alyssa turning into a giant pit bull terrier and gnawing my arm off, and I had another dream where Hubert was screaming at me in Chinese, from the top of a water tower.

I felt like I was sleepwalking, getting ready for school. I slipped Harry a couple of dog biscuits and then had to fake a coughing attack to cover up the crunching.

On Bleecker Street, with only a few minutes left of Harry and my father sharing the same territory, Jane started to sing, to the tune of "Mary Had a Little Lamb."

> *"Billie had a little dog,*
> *Little dog, little dog,*
> *Billie had a little dog,*
> *Its fur would never show. . . ."*

"Jane." I kept my voice even. She would not feel any need for loyalty if I were beating her up, which is what I wanted to do. My father commented that there was nothing better than a bright October day. So far, he was not paying attention to us.

> *"It followed her to school one day,*
> *School one day, school one day,*

It followed her to school one day,
But no one would ever know."

"Jane," I said, trying to imitate that special tone that the principal uses to stop kids from running in the hall.

She stopped singing to concentrate on side-stepping somebody else's dog's poop, and then looked up at me with the smile of an innocent angel.

"Yes, Sister Dearest?" she inquired.

"Consider yourself face-paintless, as well as strangled, if you so much as peep."

Jane glanced at my father, who was three or four steps ahead of us, actually whistling! Because the sun was shining and he was taking the morning off work, using fatherly duty as an excuse.

"Woof," said Jane.

I squinted at my demon sister and drew a finger across my throat.

We got to school before I killed her.

Hubert was waiting on the steps. My father took Jane and started in.

"I'll come to your class and wave good-bye," he said to me. "I haven't seen George Donaldson in a couple of years."

I wasn't listening. Soon we'd we safely inside.

"Bye, Dad." I opened the door for Hubert. So far, so good.

"Did you bring the gum?" I asked him in a low voice. "Let's go, right now. We still have time. We can do it in the cafeteria bathroom. No one's down there in the morning."

"Billie," said Hubert. Something was wrong.

"What?"

"There's a problem. They rescheduled the medieval pageant. We're doing it now, for the whole Lower School, now, this morning, in the auditorium, instead of this afternoon, because the radiators are having emergency surgery at two o'clock."

"Oh, sh-sh-shoelace!" I yelped. "How could this happen to us?"

"Mr. D. is getting everybody into their costumes right now."

We grumbled our way to join the rest of the

class, with Harry's baby snores coming out of my pack. He was getting used to riding around on my back, and usually nodded off after a few minutes of real motion.

"He hasn't eaten, except dog biscuits, since we were at your house. I haven't had a chance to feed him the last can of food. Oh, and Jane knows about him."

"Oh, great!" said Hubert. "The large-mouth bass!"

That's why I like Hubert. He understands about siblings without even having one.

Upstairs was chaos.

Our classroom was the girls' changing room, and the other sixth grade across the hall was for the boys.

Over in the corner, next to the fish tank, I fluffed my jacket into a cushion and settled the sleeping Harry.

My costume was supposed to look like a minstrel sort of a person. I had blue leggings and a green tunic and a pretend lute that I'd made in shop.

Suddenly there was a mass squeal. I spun around to see my father's face grinning into the room.

"Dad!" I screamed. "This is the changing room! We're getting ready for the pageant! Get out!"

"Ooops!" he said, chuckling as he closed the door.

I was burning with embarrassment. Nobody else's father would do such a thing.

"Hmmm," murmured Alyssa for the general audience. "Billie's father is a Peeping Tom."

"Oh, shut up, Alyssa!" I hissed. She always found the very worst thing to say.

I could see my dad through the door window, hugging Mr. Donaldson in one of those men's back-slapping hugs. Maybe they'd been friends, back when my parents were still married. I'd never thought about that part, about how my dad was separated from his whole old life, as well as his wife and children.

I had most of my costume on. Harry was still asleep. I slipped into the hall to hear what was happening. And just at that minute, Jane showed up, too, waving and chattering.

"Hello, there," said Mr. Donaldson in his jovial way. "Aren't you supposed to be in the auditorium?"

"Katie's saving me a seat in the front row," said Jane. "But I'm supposed to tell you, everybody's waiting."

"You're staying to watch this, aren't you, Alex?" Mr. D. asked my dad.

"I wouldn't miss it for the world," said my father, acting like he'd been up all night on the ticket line. He winked at me and went down to find a seat, followed by most of the sixth grade, clinking their chain mail and waving banners. The stragglers were just coming out of the classroom.

"You look pretty, Billie," said Jane, following me as I looked for my hood and cowl. "But what are you going to do with the puppy while the pageant is going on? Can I hold him?"

Of course, Alyssa had to be the one to overhear.

"What are you talking about, you little

weirdo?" she asked. "You don't have a puppy."

Across the room, I could see the indentations in my jacket shifting as Harry woke up and stretched his legs.

"Yeah, well, we do have a puppy," I retorted. "He just happens to be invisible."

19 • Double-Dose Revenge

Jane stared at me in surprise, but Alyssa just snorted. It was the funniest thing she'd ever heard.

"You are such a liar, Billie Stoner, and you're teaching your brat sister to be just like you."

"She is not," Jane shouted, going right up to Alyssa and shaking her fist. "She's the smartest and the bravest and the telling-truthest of anybody."

"Yeah, and she needs a six-year-old to stick up for her," Alyssa sneered, pushing Jane out of the way. She clutched her wimple and clomped down the stairs in her medieval footwear, which was actually her mother's beach sandals.

Megan and Emma and Max rustled after her in their paper tabards, bearing lances and shields.

It was those sandals that gave me my next good idea. Jane and I were the only ones left.

"You go ahead, Jane," I said. "I have to get my hood on. Hey, and thanks for yelling at Alyssa. That almost makes up for being such a dodo the rest of the time." She beamed with happiness and headed off obediently.

I fished one of Alyssa's prized platform shoes from under her desk. It was made of something that looked like blue rubber corduroy.

I dangled it in the air, just above nose level for a frisky puppy.

"Here you go, Harry," I said, with heartfelt encouragement. He tugged it out of my fingers at once.

"Have a good chew."

I closed the door carefully behind me.

The pageant was a huge success. At least the audience thought so; they especially liked the jousting match and the mummers' dance. Mr. Donaldson was proud of us, and only two costumes (Nick's and Emma's) got torn and only one shield (Sarah's) got sat on and crushed. Jane kept waving at me and cheering, and my dad stood in the back, winking whenever I looked at him.

Right at the end, I got the giggles, thinking about Alyssa's shoe. Afterward, while the teachers were pouring out cider and serving a "medieval feast" of ginger cookies and Fig Newtons and almonds and raisin mix, I raced upstairs to check the damage.

The floor beside Alyssa's desk was awash with shreds of blue rubber. I hoped poor Harry hadn't swallowed any of that stuff; it was probably toxic. He'd abandoned the shoe carcass, still intact except for its skin, and moved on to the wastepaper basket, which now had tooth marks all around the rim.

I heard noises in the stairwell.

"Harry! Here, boy!" I held out the cookie I'd snatched from the feast.

He pounced on me in delight, eating greedily.

"You were hungry, weren't you, Harry? That shoe just didn't satisfy."

I felt his warm tongue and watched my fingers disappear at the same instant.

"Uh-oh, no more of that," I said, scooping him up and tucking him, wriggling, under one arm. "We have a mission."

Leaving my clothes till later, I collected my backpack full of potion ingredients and got through the door just as Hubert and Charley reached the top of the stairs. Together they were dressed as a dragon (killed during the pageant by fearless knights). Hubert was the back half.

"C'mon, Hubert. Remove thy tail," I said. "Bring the gum and meet me you-know-where."

"Oooooh," teased Charley, clasping the dragon's head under his arm. "Sounds nasty!"

Hubert flushed, but he obeyed.

The stairs were filling up with kids as everyone headed up to change. I passed Alyssa, holding my breath.

Less than a minute later, a violent scream shook the walls, and everyone stood still in alarm. Except me, of course. I knew the source, and I was biting my lip not to laugh out loud as I bounded for the exit.

Escape was not quite so easy.

In the main hall, my father and Mr. Donaldson were still chatting away like baby-sitters on a park bench.

"Billie, great show!" My father applauded. "I'll tell you what. I'm going to ask Mr. Donaldson here for permission to take my daughter out to lunch."

Mr. Donaldson smiled and actually ruffled my hair!

"Uh, Dad, I don't know, it's not . . ." Harry was really starting to struggle in my arms.

"Oh, come on, sweetie, I never get to hang out around the school. I'll take you to Pizza Box. I'll meet you out front in, what? Twenty minutes?"

He glanced at Mr. D. for confirmation. "Twenty minutes. Will that give you time to get changed out of thirteenth-century gear? I'll go get Jane. Oh, and ask Hubert, too."

"Sure, Dad," I said.

Hubert was suddenly at my elbow.

"Billie, what happened upstairs?" he asked. "Alyssa is foaming at the mouth."

Mr. Donaldson raised an eyebrow and headed straight for the stairs.

"Twenty minutes, Billie," said my dad as he followed Mr. D.

Hubert and I speed-walked to the bathroom, almost getting there safely.

"Billie!"

Alyssa's screech followed me into the girls' room. Because there was a furious female on his tail, Hubert couldn't come in with me. I guessed he would lurk in the hall until the coast was clear. I could finally put Harry down. He immediately gave the warning growl that I'd learned to dread.

Alyssa came slamming through the door, hobbling on her shoes. One of them was as bright and rubbery as the day they arrived in the mail, and the other one looked like soggy cardboard.

"I don't know how you did this," Alyssa said in a voice full of vengeance, "but I'm going to make you pay! Ewww! What's that smell?"

Harry had done his business, but there was nothing to be seen. I shrugged my shoulders.

Alyssa backed out of the room, holding her nose and giving me the evil eye.

Too bad I didn't have the satisfaction of seeing her face one minute later, but Hubert gave me a full report.

As Alyssa stalked down the hall, proclaiming loudly to the cafeteria line that Billie Stoner was a stinker, it became clear that her one blue, shiny shoe was encrusted with fresh dog poop.

I frantically cleaned up the remaining evidence and stuck my head out of the bathroom to see. Alyssa began sobbing wildly. Finally she settled down and reluctantly accepted Megan's shabby old gym shoes to wear for the afternoon.

20 • *Harry's Bath*

Hubert joined me in the girls' room, and we laughed so hard that Harry got excited and barked along with us. We had to use one of the dog biscuits from the recipe to make him quiet.

"We only have a few minutes," I reminded Hubert. "My father is threatening to humiliate me some more by taking us out to lunch."

I ran water into the sink, but it filled so quickly I knew it was nowhere near two gallons. Plus, it was so shallow that Harry could never be submerged. Maybe we'd have to sneak into the kitchen.

"How about the toilet?" asked Hubert. "It's just sitting there, full of water."

"Ready and waiting," I added. He lifted up the seat.

I unfolded the page from the phone book with the recipe scribbled around the edges.

"Water," I said.

"Check," said Hubert.

"Talcum powder."

"Check."

"Okay, this one is made of powdered goat horn," I said, pouring from the Sippy-Cup.

"Check," said Hubert.

"And this one is chrysanthemum flowers."

"Check."

"Tubers of lilyturf." I remembered that Jody had crumbled them into small chunks when she'd made the bath for me last spring.

"Yuck," said Hubert. "Check."

"Now we have to mash up the dog biscuits." I dumped the contents of the box onto the floor. I could see where Harry was by where the bits were vanishing.

Hubert and I stomped until the floor was covered with crumbs. Then we swept them up in our hands and tossed them into the toilet with the rest of the mess.

"And the gum!" Hubert reminded me. "I chewed my jaw off last night." We squeezed the gummy lumps to let the juice trickle in and then threw in the whole bagful.

Harry was panting.

"This is for you, boy," I said. "You lucky doggy." I looked around for something to stir with but ended up using my hand.

"This is completely disgusting," I said. "Now for the hard part. We have to put him in and hold him under."

I reached for Harry.

"In complete darkness," I added. "Turn off the light, would you, Hubert?"

The room went black. We were all invisible. There was a pencil line of light coming from under the door, and that was it. Black night.

I held Harry close, feeling it was the last moment that he was really mine.

Suddenly there was a pounding on the door. I clutched Harry so hard he yelped. Hubert gasped in alarm.

"Open up!" I didn't recognize the husky voice.

"Just a second!" I called out.

"What are we going to do?" hissed Hubert.

"Who do you think it is?" I hissed back.

The door handle moved. We had forgotten to turn the lock! Light from the hall fell into the room as someone pushed open the door.

"Hey, what are you doing in here with the lights off?" The voice that started out deep and gruff turned into boy laughter as Charley found more than he'd expected.

"Just tell me what you're doing with the gum!" He was choking on his own joke. Hubert about fainted with mortification, but I was just mad.

"Charley, you get out of here right now. We are having a private conference, and it's none of your nosy-parker business." Harry was struggling to get out of my hold.

"Oh, I've got to get a witness to this!" Charley exclaimed as he headed for the cafeteria.

I locked the door behind him, darkening the room back into a coal mine.

Feeling desperate, I plunged Harry into the toilet with no mercy.

He went crazy, barking and flapping and even snarling.

"I'm sorry, honey," I kept saying. "I'm sorry. We've got about twelve seconds before they knock down the door. You're going to feel better, I promise. Hubert! Help me! I'm getting soaked!"

Harry thrashed and yipped while I tried to get the sludge on his head and over his ears and around the tail.

I rubbed it deep into his fur, pretending to give him a shampoo.

"How long do we have to keep him in here?" asked Hubert.

"Let's check now. Hit the switch."

The room buzzed with light.

I blinked, feeling like a bat in sunshine.

And then I saw Harry.

"He's here!"

Harry was sodden and miserable but all here.

I lifted him out of the toilet and rubbed him all over with paper towels, until his fur stood up and most of the bath lumps were gone. He was even cuter than I remembered.

"Wow," whispered Hubert in awe. "We really did it!"

"We did it!" I hollered, loud and happy. We jumped up and down, punching each other with glee. Harry, of course, began to bark.

"Okay, stop." I took a deep breath. "We have to hurry. We've got to clean up this mess and, oh my God, look at you!"

Hubert's T-shirt was wet through, and his arms were coated in crud.

"You should talk, Billie. Your hair looks like it's full of vomit."

I checked the mirror and groaned.

"Do you think it's safe to flush the toilet?" asked Hubert. We stood shoulder to shoulder examining the porcelain bowl full of slops.

I skimmed a couple of handfuls off the top and delivered them to the garbage can.

"We can only try," I said, pushing on the lever.

Harry lifted his front paws onto the rim and watched with curiosity as the soup swirled and the pipes gagged and choked. Finally, thankfully, everything was sucked down.

We mopped the floor with more paper towels. Hubert splashed off his arms and squeezed what he could out of his shirt.

I twisted my head upside down in the sink, trying to rinse my hair, but mostly I sprayed water on the wall.

Harry suddenly shook himself, showering our knees and ankles, as if he'd just learned to be a real dog. From head to foot, I was various stages from damp to saturated.

The doorknob jiggled, and there was another knock.

"Billie! Charley said you were in there. Come out right now." It was my little sister.

21 • *Dénouement*

Come on!" Jane called. "Daddy is waiting outside, and so is that Jody girl."

I flicked the lock and opened the door. Jane stared.

Harry greeted her with two happy barks.

"He's real!" she exclaimed, crouching to pet him. "How did you do that? And why are you all wet? And why is Hubert in the bathroom with you?"

"Let's go," I said.

I picked up Harry and cradled him in my arms, feeling sadness settle over me like dust.

Jody was here to collect Harry. I was minutes away from having to say good-bye.

Sure enough, out on the school steps, Dad

and Jody were chatting together like old friends.

Harry nearly jumped from my grasp as he spotted Sam being yanked toward us by his company of dogs.

"Yo! Shortie!" Sam hailed me.

"Yo," I said weakly.

Jody reached over to pet Harry. "Hey! Harry! Nice to see ya!" And then, in a whisper, "Is that Sam? He's totally cute."

The dogs greeted one another with a chorus of barks and yaps.

"Jody!" I shouted over the noise. "How was the science competition?"

"Oh, I won," she announced, trying to be cool. Then her face split in a silver smile. "It was mighty."

"You're Jody?" asked Sam. "You're the whiz kid?" He looked impressed.

"Congratulations, Jody!" said my father. "Whatever you won, I'm sure you deserved it." He was trying to talk normally, but he was surrounded by large, sniffing dogs. His ankles must give off some enticing scent. Jane begged the leads from Sam, and they were soon hopelessly tangled.

A taxi pulled up at the curb.

"Yikes!" said Hubert.

My mother climbed out.

Jane dropped all the leashes to hurl herself at Mom. The barking doubled as the dogs realized they were free and tried to pull apart.

"Quite a reception!" laughed my mother, hanging on to Jane and tugging her bag out of the cab at the same time.

Sam and Jody called the dogs firmly to attention and sorted out the leads, while Harry watched, panting.

"Welcome back, Mary," said my father.

She gave him a cheerful, polite smile. It was hard to believe they had ever been madly in love.

"Thanks for taking the girls, Alex," said my mother.

I could hardly bear to watch them, even though I was dying to. They were hardly ever together to provide this dilemma.

My mother focused on me.

"You're dressed for the pageant already! But why are you wet?"

"The pageant's over, Mommy," Jane said, as if that explained everything. "They did it this morning."

Harry chose that moment to start licking my face.

"And who's this?" my mother asked.

I felt myself fill up with sudden, electric resolve. It was now or never.

"Mom, this is Harry. He's, well, he's—"

"Hello, Ms. Stoner, I'm Jody," said Jody, extending her hand, with professional good manners. "My dog, Pepper, is Harry's mother."

"Oh, you must be Hubert's friend." My mother remembered my lie after Jody's original phone call.

"And I'm Sam," said Sam, extending his hand. "I work for Billie."

My mother's eyes drilled into mine.

"Mom." I cleared my throat.

"Can we keep Harry, Mommy? Please, pretty please?" Jane jumped to the punch line.

My mother's eyebrows went up. She put her bag down.

"Mom," I said again, "I've been doing Jody a favor while she tries to find homes for her puppies. But I want it to be us who gives Harry a home. And before you say anything, I've had Harry since Saturday night, and—"

My mother shot a look of irritation at Dad. "Oh, Alex, how could you? You have the common sense of a, of a puppy dog! We agreed we would discuss—"

"Mom!" I interrupted. "You're not letting me tell you! You're just flipping out at Dad instead of listening to me. I'm the person who's talking to you. I'm the person you live with!"

There was silence.

"You're right, Billie. But it's my house. Don't I get to choose how many . . . living creatures I have to look after?"

"But you don't have to look after him. That will be my job. With some help from Sam. And Jane," I added quickly.

"I'll tell you the truth, Mary," my father said placidly. "These kids did such a good job looking after him this weekend, I hardly even knew he was there."

Jane prodded my back. "He didn't know at all!" she whispered.

"Just go along," I muttered back. "He believes his own story. He doesn't want to admit he didn't notice."

Jody was talking to Mom. "I've been very impressed with Billie's, um, intuition about Harry," she said with a straight face. "I think she's a true animal friend."

"I gotta say," said Sam suddenly, "I never knew an eleven-year-old kid who was smart enough to hire a dog walker before. And you can't send him back now. I got him a present."

Sam dipped his hand into his jeans and pulled out a collar. A red leather collar with a medallion on it, engraved with an H.

"Oh, Sam," I gasped. It was the most beautiful thing I'd ever seen.

"Cool," said Hubert.

"Wow," said Jody.

Jody and Sam looked at each other like Archie and Veronica in the comic books. I could practically see the little hearts spinning around their heads.

"So, Mary?" prodded my father.

I used my final ploy. "Can we make a deal, Mom? Can we have a trial period? And if I do a good job, for a month, or something, I can keep him?"

My mother sighed. She reached out to touch my hair and let her hand fall gently onto Harry's head. I should have thought of that before. As soon as she felt his silky ears, and his curious nose, her heart would bump just like mine did.

"Okay, honey. I'll give you a month."

Jane squealed and jumped up and down. Hubert slapped me on the back. Sam and Jody said "Yes!" in unison, clenching their fists in triumph. My father gave her a thumbs-up sign.

She smiled at us all, with her warm, crinkly-eyed smile.

"Let's just see what happens," she said.

"You won't even know we have him, Mom," I promised. "It will be just like he's invisible."

Epilogue

Okay, the bad part is that I had to buy Alyssa a new pair of ugly shoes from Delia's, using my birthday savings. The good part is she hasn't spoken to me since.

But Sam I see every day. Harry stays home when we leave in the morning. Sam has the keys and picks him up later. Harry plays with the other dogs on the route, and then Sam delivers him to me after school.

Sam and Jody have been to the movies twice together, and they walk Pepper with Sam's clients every Saturday in Central Park. This weekend, I'm going to take Harry uptown for a reunion with his mother. My mom is going to take Jane to the zoo, and I'm just going to, you know, hang out with the big kids.

My mom and dad are trying to be better with each other. We even all had supper together after Jane's recorder recital, and nobody said a single mean thing. I've read enough magazines to know that only movie stars marry each other twice, so I'm not holding out for that. But it would be nice if my parents could have a conversation. We'll never be a family living in the same house again, but I think we'll be pieces of a family that still connect sometimes.

The best thing is that Harry's trial period is over. It is hard work taking care of someone smaller than you, but it is *so* worth it. Even Hubert agrees that Harry is the cutest dog. And I added him to my personal coat of arms. My mother has said that he can be mine forever.